The Boy with a Wish

The Nicholas Stories #1

Written by Harry B. Knights
Illustrated by Calico World Entertainment

PELICAN PUBLISHING COMPANY
Gretna 2002

In memory of Andrea Barce
Her courage, her grace, her smile touched the lives
of those who knew and loved her.

First published by Zweig Knights Publishing Corporation
Published by arrangement with Zweig Knights Publishing Corporation by
    Pelican Publishing Company, Inc., 2002

The word "Pelican" and the depiction of a pelican are trademarks of Pelican Publishing
Company, Inc., and are registered in the U.S. Patent and Trademark Office.

ISBN: 1-58980-059-1

Library of Congress Cataloging-in-Publication Data

Knights, Harry B.
        The Nicholas Stories: The Boy With A Wish.
            p. cm.
Summary: A simple gift of love by a boy named Nicholas is seen by Angels, and his wish is a lasting
reward that affects the world forever.

[1. Christmas—Fiction. 2. Santa Claus—Fiction.
 3. The North Pole—Fiction 4. Religion—Inspirational. 5. Family Values—Fiction]
 1. Title.

Printed in Korea

Published by Pelican Publishing Company, Inc.
1000 Burmaster Street, Gretna, Louisiana 70053

Prologue

Throughout the history of time, certain events have taken place that were so important that they affect our lives today. The first Christmas was one of those "Special Events", where the greatest love anyone could possibly imagine was demonstrated.

The angels, rejoicing, looked down and took notice of another selfless act of love and giving by a boy named Nicholas. This made the angels smile. It was decided that the boy's only wish would be granted, and mankind was forever changed.

This is the story of Nicholas, "The Boy With A Wish". I know it's true, because I was there....the whole time.

Mouka

In the far off Land of Yon, there lived a boy named Nicholas. He lived in a village that was so high on a mountain it snowed all year long. For most of the children, this snow was great fun to play in. But for Nicholas, it was not.

You see, Nicholas was just like all of the other children except for one thing—he could not use his legs. He could not walk or run or jump. Still, everything else was the same. He never understood why the other children treated him differently. He had four brothers and three sisters who were all very nice to him. But still, when it came to playing outside, the children in the village played without Nicholas.

One day on his birthday, his father gave him a wonderful sled. He had built it himself and made the sled so Nicholas could sit on it and push himself around using his hands. To make the sled even better, his father had carved the boy's name down the middle of the sled. It read "NICHOLAS". The sled was a perfect gift. Finally, Nicholas could go out and play with the other children.

Each day, his mother helped him bundle up for
the cold snowy weather and off he would go.

Still, nobody chose him to be on their side for the snowball war. When the great snowman was to be made, he was not invited to help. And so it went. The sled was truly a great gift, but being able to go out with the other children did not mean being allowed to join them.

It was not uncommon to see him looking out a window of his family's cottage and "POW"........ a snowball would hit the window and Nicholas would naturally jump.

This made the children laugh, but it made Nicholas very, very sad.

While his mother was baking bread and other mouth-watering delights, Nicholas watched his father who was busy making shoes and boots, for he was a cobbler. Sometimes, he would let Nicholas help him and soon, Nicholas became very good at making things.

Nobody in the village had very much money and so there were not many toys for the children. He soon began fixing broken toys and dolls for his brothers and sisters. Many of these toys were even better than when they were new.

Nicholas had an idea. He decided to find as many broken and unwanted toys and dolls as he could. He would fix them up to be even better than new. Then, when one of the children in the village would have a birthday, he would leave one of those magnificent gifts at their front door.

This, of course made the children very happy. Seeing the children so happy made Nicholas feel very, very good. Soon people from other villages heard of the boy with the gifts and asked him to help their children as well.

This kept him so busy that he soon ran out of broken toys and he started making new toys out of whatever things he could find. He still was not invited out to play, but it no longer mattered. Nicholas enjoyed making children happy and that was all that he wished to do.

Then one day, a man came to visit him.

He told Nicholas about his little girl named Kristina who lived in a village on the other side of the mountain. She had very few friends because she was born unable to hear. This made it difficult for her to speak and the other children made fun of her and teased her. These children just did not realize how badly they made Kristina feel. In a few days she was going to have a birthday, but she had become very ill with a fever.

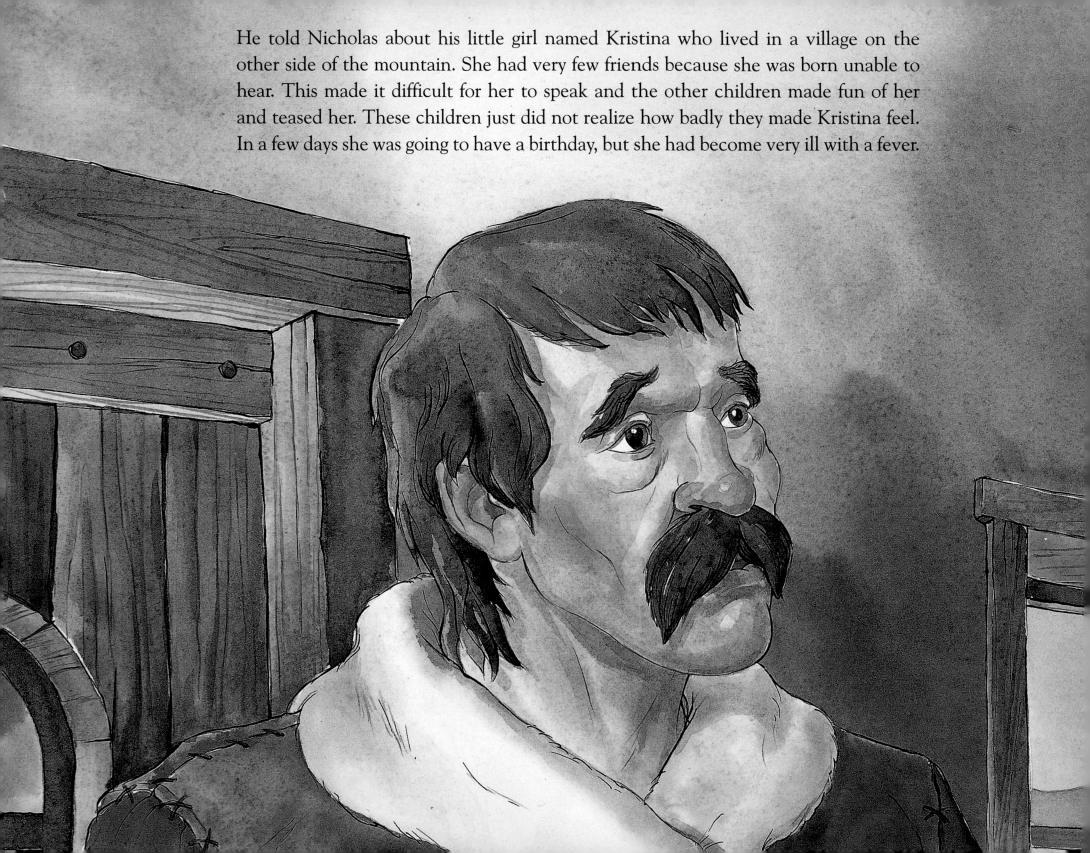

Her family had very little money and was not able to buy her the doll that she wished for so much. Her father knew that a beautiful doll would make her feel better and asked if Nicholas would help. Nicholas, of course, promised he would.

During the next two days he worked very hard to make the most beautiful doll ever for the little girl.

Finally, it was ready just in time for Kristina's birthday. He thought of how happy she would be when she saw it.

When Nicholas looked outside, he realized it was snowing. Not just any snowstorm mind you, but a really, really big snowstorm. In fact, it was the biggest storm he had ever seen. Nicholas needed someone to take the doll to Kristina for her birthday. After all, he had made a promise.

He asked his father first, but his father was too busy making boots, and his mother was preparing dinner. His brothers and sisters were much too busy playing in the new snow. Nicholas asked, but no one was willing to help deliver the doll.

Still, there was no way that Nicholas would let Kristina wake up without her doll, so he decided to go himself. He had never been to the other side of the mountain before, but he was sure he could do it. So, he carefully wrapped the doll to protect it from the storm.

Then he left the village and made his way up the trail on his sled with Kristina's doll. The storm was getting worse, but he pushed on.

As darkness approached, he found Kristina's cottage and he carefully placed the doll at her front door and then he started back home. He was getting very, very tired and he was getting very, very cold.

Finally, he reached the top of the mountain and he knew that the most difficult part of the journey was over. As he started down the slope he lost his way in the almost total darkness with the snow whirling and blowing around him.. The cold snow crunched beneath his sled and branches clapped above his head.

He began to slide down a very steep hill and the sled went faster and faster and Nicholas could not slow it down. Faster and faster and faster he went. Down, down, down the mountain. The snow stung his face as the trees raced by him.

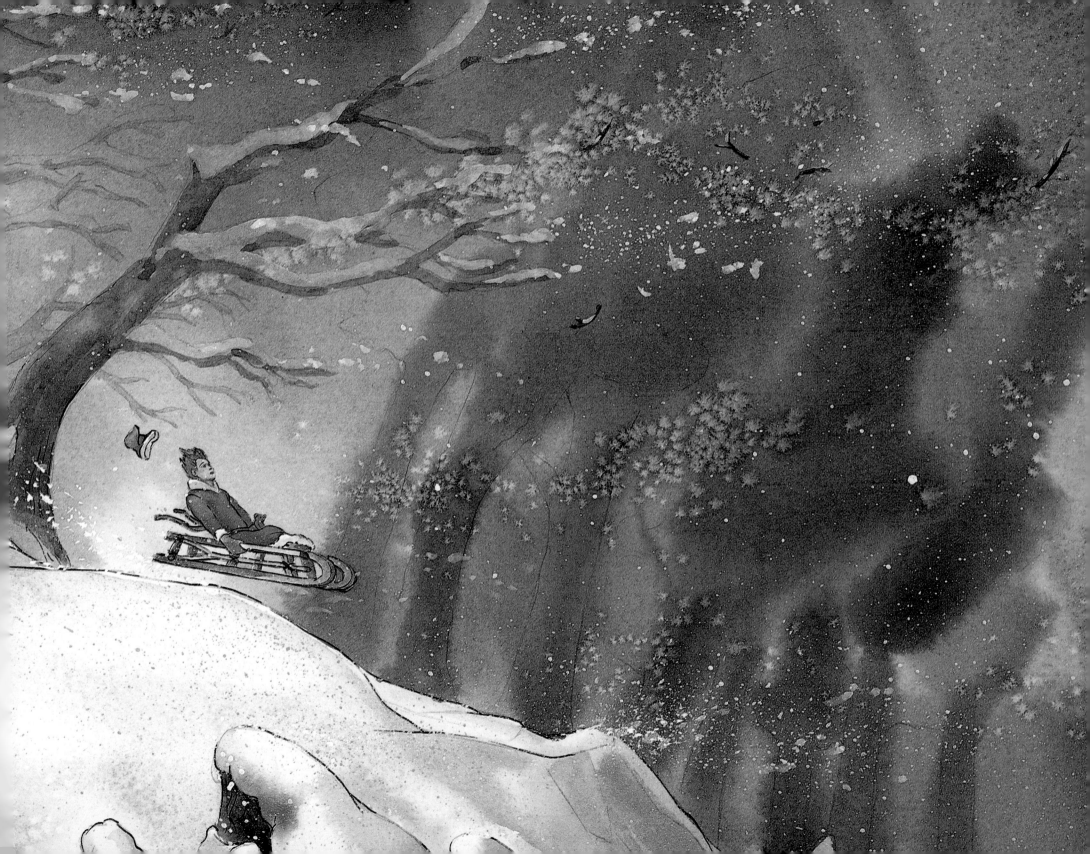

The cold wind and blowing snow stole all feeling from the boy as his sled flew down the mountain, and all of a sudden, there was total silence. His journey, it seemed, was now over.

His family wondered where he could be. As darkness had approached, they searched for him, going from door to door. More and more people joined the search, but still, no Nicholas.

Nearly every man, woman, and child from every village around tried to find the boy with a wish, but they never found him. They knew then what a special friend they had lost. Oh, how they wished they had been kinder to him!

What they did not know however, was what a glorious thing had happened to Nicholas. Soon after there was total silence, he then saw what appeared to be a Bright Light. It was a beautiful sight, full of love and all the happiest thoughts anyone could possibly imagine. Nicholas had never felt so well in his whole entire life. It was then that he realized he was standing on his own two feet. There were no crutches, no sled...just his very own two feet.

Then he heard a wonderful voice, the kind of voice that an angel might have. Nicholas Kringle was told that he was very special because he possessed the gift of love: always giving, always loving, no matter what.

Nicholas was reminded that a very special *Child* had been born many years ago. That special *Child's* birthday was called *Christmas*. In order for the *Child's* birthday to be remembered forever and always, it was decided that Nicholas would be granted his wish to make children happy. He was told that he would travel the whole world every year on the night before *Christmas* and leave a gift for every girl and boy. This would fulfill the boy's wish by making all the children happy. It would also help the children remember the *Child's* birthday forever and always.

Nicholas asked, "How will this be possible? After all, there are so many children!"

The answer was simple. He was given the gift of Time. He was told "You may take as much Time as you need to make the deliveries. No matter how much Time you take, it will still be the night before *Christmas*. Remember, all things are possible if you believe."

Well, he did believe, and "*The Boy With A Wish*" became known as "*Saint Nicholas*".